A MAGIC CIRCLE BOOK

Dancing Nadine

story and pictures by **ARNOLD CLAPMAN**

THEODORE CLYMER
SENIOR AUTHOR, READING 360

GINN AND COMPANY
A XEROX EDUCATION COMPANY

Home Office, Lexington, Massachusetts 02173

Library of Congress Catalog Card Number: 72-76535

International Standard Book Number: 0-663-25480-9

This is Nadine who loves to dance.

She dances outside in the daytime.

And she dances inside at night.

Sometimes she dances for her friends.

Here comes a friend now.

"Hello," says Nadine.
"I will do a dance for you."

She does a dance of the grass

and of birds

of trees

and of the sky!

At night Nadine must say good-by
and go to sleep inside her house.
Her dance is ended.

But her friend is remembering dancing Nadine.

And he, too, feels like dancing.

He does a dance of fresh air and springtime

and ponds filled with bugs

of ripe berries and wiggly worms

of slow streams and open woods

and of the long winter sleep

all safe and warm in his shell.

Good night.

ABCDEFGHIJK 765432
PRINTED IN THE UNITED STATES OF AMERICA